First Little Readers™ E

Gabby Loves Green

by Liza Charlesworth

ISBN: 978-1-338-29787-4

Illustrated by Tammie Lyon

First printing, June 2018.

This is Gabby.
Guess what?

Gabby loves green.
Green, green, green!

Gabby loves to play
with green toys.
She plays with a green ball.

Then she plays
with a green robot.

Gabby loves to paint
green pictures.
She paints a green tree.

Then she paints
a green monster.

Gabby loves to eat
green food.
She eats a green salad.

Then she eats
a green cupcake.

Gabby loves to hold
green animals.
She holds a green frog.

Then she holds
a green snake.

Gabby loves to put on
green clothes.
She puts on a green dress.

Then she puts on
a green crown.

Then she puts on
big green glasses.
Guess what?

The big green glasses
make everything green.

Green, green, green!
Gabby loves green.